I0618380

A Favorite Son

USA Today

Bestselling Author

UVI POZNANSKY

Published by Uviart
P.O. Box 3233 Santa Monica CA 90408
Blog: uviart.blogspot.com
Email: uvi.author@gmail.com

First Edition 2013
Printed in the United States of America
Book design, cover design, and cover image by
Uvi Poznansky

Contents

Chapter 1
Lentil Stew

At birth—thanks to my twin brother Esav who, on his way out, pushed me back into the womb—I missed the chance, unfortunately, of becoming the First Born son. My mother told me that I missed it by no more than a split second. I often wonder why she shared this detail with me.

Perhaps she wanted to draw me closer, or else she could not foresee—how could she, really—the ways in which it would affect me.

The disclosure filled my heart with hate, bitter hate for my brother, and stirred a good measure of resentment in me, because of being seen by everyone around me as inferior to him. A split second was all it took to rob me of my future. It set before me a risky path—a path to failure, to oblivion—and turned me, from birth, into a loser.

I spent the rest of my life souring over it.

And not just souring, mind you: I was constantly calculating, searching for ways to take it back, take his birthright away from him. Despite our closeness, or maybe because of it, I felt a burning desire to surpass my brother. So, even before I knew what a birthright was, and how much power, honor, wealth it could bestow upon you, I had a pressing need to claim it.

The First Born son! It came to mean everything for me: The upper hand in life! The inheritance in full: Herds, camels, women, gold coins! And above all—taking over my father's position and, in time, becoming the leader, the rightful head of the family. I had to win it all—or else be left with nothing.

If not the First Born son, I might as well be a bastard. And so, in my quest for legitimacy, I knew I had to betray my brother. I had to fool my father. What I failed to predict was the formation of a hole in my life. How could I expect loneliness.

I underestimated its weight. To my astonishment, it grows heavier and more burdensome now, with every passing year.

It all started, innocently enough, with a meal. A real meal, I mean, made with a fresh kill over a roaring fire, under the open sky—not one that is made with stored, half-cooked cuts of meat and reheated, somehow, in a stuffy restaurant kitchen, the likes of which can be found down over there, along the inhabited, coastal regions of Canaan, near the city of Ashdod. Luckily none of those establishments can be found here, at the frontier of this desert, which is where our camp is set.

Don't let them fool you. Anyone can barbecue a steak—but really, cooking a stew is another matter altogether. The pot must be simmering for several hours. And so, from time to time you must drizzle in some water, which in this wasteland is nearly impossible to come by. Most wells around here are bone-dry, or else fiercely guarded, and rarely shared by other tribes.

Next you must find a well-trained chef. So let me assure you, son: There is no soul in the entire world, or at least in these parts, in Canaan, with a better nose than mine. Yankle's nose— no one comes close!

A Favorite Son

When I sprinkle my secret blend of spices—here, take a sniff, can you smell it? When I chop these mouthwatering sun-dried tomatoes, add a few cloves of garlic for good measure, and let it all sizzle with lentils and meat—it becomes so scrumptious, so lip-smacking, finger-licking, melt-in-your-mouth good!

There is a certain ratio of flavors, a balance that creates a feast for the tongue and a delight for the mind. And having mastered that balance, with a pinch of imported cumin from the north of Persia, a dash of saffron from the south of Egypt, I can tell you one thing: when the pot comes to a full bubbling point, and the aroma of the stew rises up in the air—it would make you dribble! Drive you to madness! For a single bite, you would sell your brother, if only you had one!

I hear no arguments from you. Of course, your mouth is full! Here, here's a napkin. There, there, wipe your chin.

You would sell me your land, or your camels, or your birthright as the First Born—even if you had no idea what in the world that could mean, which, oddly enough, is exactly what my brother did.

Long ago I used to look up to him. He used to chase birds and I used to chase him. We could finish each other's sentences. We were so close! Close enough for him to sense exactly what I thought, which was this: if I just pushed myself a little harder, or else if I pushed him aside, I could, perhaps, outpace him by a nose—which, for me, would be a measure of victory.

I remember how I used to follow him around, never too far behind him, a flesh of his flesh—until the time came when he grew away from me, grew into something that was quite out of my reach: A hunter. His leg muscles became stronger than mine, and so he could leap higher from one rock to another. To my dismay I found myself falling behind, which made me so resentful, so envious of him, that hairy schmuck!

He is as dumb as he is big. At times I suspect he blames me for all his misfortunes, or maybe he blames my stew. But to be honest—which sometimes I am—I think he slipped into his own drool. He should blame no one else but himself, nothing else but his own greed.

Did I tell you it all started with a meal? I will never forget that fateful evening. It is so vivid in my mind as if it has just happened.

I have just added some dry branches to sustain the fire, so that the pot would go on simmering nicely. Then I turn around and go back inside, planning to do nothing more than sit idly in my tent and dream. There is nothing to watch, out there, but the tired sight of sunset, a stretch of sky dimming over the parched, barren land. Sand, sand and sand, as far as the eye can see. And then—listen!—out of the blue, I hear a heavy thump of footsteps.

The thump gets louder. It is growing more deafening by the second, and before you know it, a dark outline falls upon the canvas of my tent.

I can tell it is my brother, by the way the silhouette of his body is fused with his arrows. Without bothering to untie the flaps of my tent, and without waiting for an invitation, in he comes, bringing with him a cloud of dust and a pungent smell of sweat. For some reason, he looks at me with a hard, wolfish glint.

"Welcome," I say, jumping to my feet and, on the spot, taking a step back.

"Aha," says he, breathing heavily.

"Aha? How do you mean, Aha?" I say, trying to gauge, in the space of that second, the hunger in his eyes.

"Aha you," he counters. "Man must hunt, all alone. No help from little brother. Understand? That Aha."

"Well, mom says I'm too young."

"Aha. You my age."

"Even so. I'm a split second younger, aren't I? She wouldn't let me go hunting."

"Mom says. Mom says. You in her tent, always."

"Are you jealous?" I tease him. "I can't believe it!"

To which he roars, "You do nothing, you! You cook, you hide. Coward! Aha, coward you!"

He takes one step forward, I take two back. The arrows slung over his shoulder clink against each other. It is a steely, menacing sound. With one blow of his hand, he smacks down the canvas, and on the double the entire tent is flattened into a lopsided mess, collapsing upon itself, its pegs flying clear out, bouncing over and over, over the soft sand.

He gets in my face. We are standing nose to nose. The moment I have dreaded all my life is suddenly upon me, and there is no way to withdraw. I have to face him, which forces me to examine him closely. To my surprise, I notice how terribly exhausted he is. His face is pale, his breath tormented, his tongue dry—all of which gives me hope: I may yet come out of this alive.

How can I possibly foresee, at that moment, that what happens next would surpass even my wildest dreams?

Just before he shoulders me aside, I get hold, somehow, of one of his arrows. "Really," I say, whipping him to a standstill with the arrow. "I can sure learn a thing or two from my big brother, now can I? You're the Hunter. You're the Man!"

"I am," says he, but in a flash the wind goes out of him.

I can see, plain as can be, that an amazing transformation is coming upon him: one minute—he towers over me, a beast with bushy eyebrows and an inflated chest, dense with hair; the next —he's flat at my feet, like a fleecy rug of fur. Faint with hunger, dizzy with thirst, here is my brother: A giant kneeling before me over what remains of my tent. In spite of myself I feel for him, which is an unusual feeling for me to have. It stays with me for the duration of a full minute.

"You must be tired," I say, with a tinge of acid in my voice. "Tough day at work? Nothing to show for, after eight hours of hunt?"

He gives a heartbreaking sigh. "Ah ha..."

"You don't look so good."

"Huh?"

I lean over, try to hug him, revive him, or at least hear his words—but to no avail: His lips are cracked, his whisper— incoherent. Yet, I know what he needs: A gulp of water.

We have not been camping close to a well for nearly three days now—but I happen to know where water can be found, because in her tent, under her bed, my mother keeps a full jug, for no one else but me. And so, I bring it to him, catching myself in an unexpectedly generous mood. He takes a long gulp. Then he has to catch his breath.

"Yankle?" he says.

"Yes, Esav?"

"What is this smell? So good..."

"It's my new recipe! I call it *a stew*."

"Give me. Give me now!"

"Well, no," I say. "There are limits to my generosity."

"You be sorry," says he.

"Well, what's in it for me?"

"Huh?"

"Do I really have to explain? What will you give me in return?"

"Give you?" he flares up. "A big smack."

"Oh well." I laugh in his face. "Forget it, then."

He falls to some deep thoughts, by the end of which he throws his hands up in the air. "I give you something," he offers. "Anything."

I smile. "You know what I want."

Then he hesitates. "No. Not that."

Well, by now you know me: I can find a way, some way to convince him. So I go over to my big pot and, as theatrically as I can, raise the iron lid.

Out comes a puff of steam, escaping high into the air and carrying with it the most tempting, most delectable scent. Then, using my brother's arrow as a skewer, I pierce through the juiciest, most succulent piece of meat, and bring it right under his nose.

"Smell it," I say.

His snout is drawn to the skewer like metal to magnet—but then, wait a minute!—he turns his head to me. "Is Kosher?" says he.

I am so surprised that I drop the lid. "Kosher?" I say. "Who cares?"

"Dad says —"

"Dad? What does he know?"

"He study them scriptures —"

"Scriptures!" I cry. "What scriptures? Who the hell needs scriptures?"

He shrugs in confusion, and I find myself having to explain:

"Someday, some wisecracker suffering from a heatstroke in the middle of the Sinai desert will decide to write some directions in some God-awful scriptures, directions that record for posterity, in excruciating detail, a whole list of particulars about how to prepare food with a sense of *morality*, whatever the hell *that* is, namely, how to cook Kosher. I assure you, morality is nothing useful—not for you and me."

"Oh," says my brother.

"At any rate, right now there are no scriptures, and it's going to take forever—a few years, maybe decades, even centuries to write them, which will give you plenty of time to learn to read, see?"

"See," he echoes.

"In the meantime, look here." I point out with the skewer. "It's the flavor of the month! Red hot and dripping with fat..."

He starts to dribble. I have never seen his nostrils flare open to such a degree.

"Well," say I. "Don't sniff at me just because you're older. You are hungry. So am I."

By now, his eyes are bulging with greed. Clearly, he needs all his wits to escape temptation. Regrettably, all his wits do not amount to much.

"Come on!" I say. "You know exactly what I want."

His surrender is close at hand. I can almost touch it. At long last, we are on the verge of striking a deal.

"Sell me your birthright," I say, as loudly as I can. "We are twins, after all. First son, second son—same difference, right? It's a split second either way. What does it matter? Sell me the damn thing and you get to eat. That stew is waiting! I made it for you, Esav, just for you..."

I say it at the top of my voice, so that everyone can hear me. For this deal to hold, I figure I need witnesses. I must ensure that my father, who lives in the right wing of the camp, and my mother, who lives in the left one, can both hear me.

The head-servant, the maids, the shepherds, even the children must all be listening in on us, even if at the moment they're cowering behind their shelters.

"All right," says my brother. His voice sinks into a whisper. "All right already."

"What?" I say. "I can't hear you!"

"Give me! Give the damn stew! Aha! The *whole* pot!" And then he adds, "The hell with you! You and your stupid birthright!"

I smile to myself, feeling as clever as can be. Now *that* is what I wanted to hear. Me and *my* stupid birthright. My, my. Mine!

He eats and eats and eats until his eyes glaze over, until the pot is empty, and its bottom scraped clean. At which time he kicks it with a vengeance. Then he staggers to his feet, turns his back and shrinks away into the night.

Later I can hear him weeping like a child in the lap of my father. I can imagine my dad, smiling upon his big boy—like he never smiled upon me—and rocking him gently to sleep, with a promise to buy him something, some nice thing in place of that which has been forever lost to him.

A split second at birth.

I admit, mine is a strange family. You might call it dysfunctional. How it became the cornerstone of multiple religions is quite beyond me. If all those believers out there are as obnoxious as I am, they should take those scriptures with a grain of salt.

And another thing: How my name became the cornerstone of that notorious chain of restaurants, which we here call, with great fondness, the *Yankle-in-the-Box* establishment, is a complete mystery to me. I guess it happened in honor of my stew. Here in the wilderness, every edible nugget—regardless of where it came from—is considered a delicacy.

I knew it the very next morning, and I still know it now: My brother hates me. He has removed me from his mind, stricken away any thought, any memory about me. I am dead to him. The scary part is, that being dead will not stand in the way of him killing me, if ever he lays eyes on me again.

It is an odd feeling. Have you ever faced it? Being dead to someone you envy, someone you miss, too. Someone who knows you intimately and, even worse, has the chutzpa to occupy your thoughts day in, day out. It grinds down on your nerves, doesn't it?

Trust me, being dead to your brother is not all that it is cracked up to be, but it does set you free—oh, don't act so surprised! It frees you from any lingering sense of obligation. Brother, you say to yourself. What does it mean, *Brother*? Nothing more than a pang, a dull pang in your heart.

You have betrayed him. Accept his hate.

You need not talk to him ever again. For the rest of your life, you are free! A *stranger*—that is what you are. A stranger, visited from time to time by dreams: Dreams about the mother you will never see again, and the father you left behind, on his deathbed. Dreams of waiting, waiting so eagerly for the next day, to meet your brother at the end of an endless exile. Dreams of grappling with him all night long, until the crack of dawn. Until your ankles give way. Until you lose your footing on the ground.

Then, rising up to take you is the darkness of the earth, which is where you wake up at sunrise to find yourself alone.

Chapter 2
The Goatskin Sleeve

My mother, you ask? She was—how shall I say it?—different. No woman among us in the camp, or out there in the grazing fields, was as captivating as her.

It was not just her beauty, nor was it the regal manner in which she carried herself, as if her tent served only as a temporary, makeshift shelter, a place to stay until the completion of some new, modern wing in an imaginary palace. If there was something that set her apart from all other women, it was her garments.

She would never wear a burka, unlike my grandmother Sarah, bless her soul, who must be turning in her grave, horrified at the thought of modesty lost. Instead of the traditional loose clothes covering the entire body, my mother adorned herself with exotic silks, bought from merchants in Damascus, which hugged her figure tightly. The silks, I mean—not the merchants.

She collected an array of translucent, sheer veils of fantastic rainbow colors, which she wore, I am told, on her wedding night. My father found it enchanting. The first time he had actually seen her face was, of course, the morning after. With the veil removed, she had fainted upon seeing him. It was not the excitement of first love. No—it must have been the corset, a tight undergarment contraption which, according to gossip, she had brought with her from the North, to keep her figure in shape.

Everyone knew she was homesick. It was no secret she would have done anything, back then, for a trip back home—but this being the middle of nowhere, far away from the towns and the settlements, out there in the densely populated regions to the west of us, there was no bus to be found. And my father insisted that a plane ticket was out of the question.

So instead, my mother decided to acquire stuff: ornamental purses of different shapes and sizes, an assortment of extravagant fur hats, imported from her faraway birthplace, and numerous pairs of snakeskin shoes with high heels, which were ill suited to the desert sand—all of which caused a stir among the local people.

I can recall how, as a child, I got a rare permission from her to come into the inner part of her tent, behind the screen, and take a peek into her chest. It was overflowing with nose rings, bracelets, and flamboyant clothes. With hesitant fingers I touched one of her shirts, which at the time, was way too big for me.

"Here, Yankle, try it on," she offered.

I did. I can still remember it: The trace of her jasmine perfume, the striped blue-on-white pattern of the weave, and the swooshing sound of the fabric as it flowed over my head and cascaded around my feet. I remember her laughter, her sudden embrace, and a heartbeat later—opening to me out of the shadow, right there behind her back—the watchful eyes of my twin brother Esav, who must have been standing there for a while, without making a sound.

How my mother sensed his presence—by what quirk of intuition she knew he had been studying us—I will never be able to guess. Perhaps she saw him in my eyes. She looked at me then with an intense look, and in a flash I learned that the unsaid can be more forceful than words. What passed between us at that moment I cannot begin to describe to you. I could hear her heart beat, and at the same instant, the same hammer was pounding in my chest.

With great calm, she gathered the garment from my hand. Then she folded it back into the chest with slow, measured movements, lowered the lid and with a clack, locked it. "Go out, Esav, go play," she said, without even bothering to turn her head, without even looking at him. And then she added softly, "You too, Yankle."

In two shakes of a lamb's tail we were outside. His hair was flowing, thick and wild, in the wind as he chased me, caught me, punched me down.

All the while, I knew: I would never forget her love, her letting me wear that unusually beautiful, striped shirt. And neither would he.

What more can I say, son? What can I tell you about my mother? She was a woman of many charms. Her clothes were striking, her footwear unconventional—but her most prized possession was a long-sleeved goatskin coat. It had a different feel, a different touch than the hide of a kid in our herds, because it came from afar, from the slopes of the snow-covered mountains in the North, where the goats, I am told, have fine, long, human-like hair.

Why my mother had brought this coat with her, why she kept it all these years, I will never know. Your guess is as good as mine. It was of no use here, in the scorching heat of this wasteland. Perhaps it reminded her of her childhood in that distant country, Harran, where the air was cooler, and the sunlight more slanted. She would often lament how far out of reach that place was. Out of reach, getting more remote and more remarkable with time, like a memory of youth.

The land there, she said, was more fertile, and the language more refined. According to her, it was the cradle of civilization.

Most winters, there was an abundance of rain, and the mud-brick homes there were taller, better insulated and less given to the wind than our flimsy tents.

Yes, she treasured that coat, and would let no one—not even me—touch it. If there was any mending to be done, she would do it herself, which caused the maidservants to raise their eyebrows.

It was kept safely in her chest, hidden from the eyes of the world, until the day came when she ripped it to shreds. I will never forget it. If I close my eyes, close them tight, then—in an instant—I can see it happening again, right here in front of me.

It is sunrise...

I awake with a start. Standing over me is the head-servant. Never before has he entered my tent without a prompt, loud greeting ahead of time. That in itself gives me a first clue that something is amiss.

"Yankle," he breathes in my ear, "wake up!"

With my eyes half open, I can tell he looks bent out of shape, more so than ever. Something, I say to myself, is definitely out of order—but I wish I can sleep it off.

Eliezer is the best butler you could wish to have. He served many masters in his time, and worked many years for grandpa Abraham, and then for my father, Isaac—but his devotion, above anyone else, lies with one person: My mother. He would move mountains for her.

Eliezer has been her confidant as long as I can remember, ever since he escorted her from her homeland, all these years ago. They traveled aboard camel backs, over the backbones of treacherous mountains and along snaking rivers. He never spoke, not even a word, about the dangers of that journey, nor about his unyielding courage to guard the young girl. He brought her here, to this wasteland, to marry his master's son, a man older than her by fifteen years: My father.

Around here, everyone seems to admire my father. True, Isaac is a wise, old man, but between me and you—dare I say it? —he is a wimp. How else can you explain him? A righteous man. A man who did nothing wrong all his life, did nothing at all, not a thing worth telling. Too much of a weakling to set out on his own journey, find his own girl, propose to her family, and give her the ride of her life by bringing her here, aboard his own camel.

Some speculate that at the time, he was undergoing some psychological counseling. Others insist he was doing nothing of the kind. At any rate, word is that he had certain—how shall we say it—problems. Something having to do with his relations, of all things, with his father. The *binding of Isaac*, people would say —but only when they think I am not listening.

Let them keep their own secrets. I'll keep mine.

A hand touches my shoulder and at once, my eyes pop open. I look up: Bending over me like a thin, fragile wire is the old head-servant, Eliezer.

"Your mother says, stop dreaming," he tells me. "She says, come quick."

The sleep lifts from my eyes. I leap to my feet and scramble over to her place.

Behind the curtain, she must have recognized my footsteps. The flaps of her tent are lifted before me by an invisible hand. I step in. Once my eyes get used to the dark interior, my mother takes hold of my shoulders and very gently, turns me around, so now I face the crack of sunlight in the canvas.

"The time has come," she whispers in my ear.

Through that crack I spot a figure out there, in the distance. Walking away from us, past the peaks of the scattered tents, way past the grazing fields, beating the dust at his heels into angry clouds, is my twin brother, Esav. His bow curves powerfully over his shoulder, and in his hand—a shining arrow.

"Look out," says my mother. "He is out for the kill."

"Well," I shrug. "What do I care. He isn't aiming at me, is he?"

"In a way, he is."

She notes the sudden confusion in my eyes. "I love you, dear, I do. But your father," she pauses for a second. "Your father is blind to reason. He has his heart set on your brother."

"What does love have to do with anything," I say, hearing the tremble in my voice. "Between Esav and me, the deal is sealed already. He is such an idiot! Such a hairy fool, to sell me his birthright. And for what, for a lentil stew? How greedy can a person be? But at this point, what's done is done. We shook hands on it! Now I am he. I am the firstborn son. Everybody knows that. Even dad."

"Really?" she says, mockingly. "But you see, to a blind man, that does not matter."

By which she means, my old man. In the span of the last six months, he has been losing his eyesight, so that by now, he is completely blind. But the way she has just said it—that inflection in her voice, that note of contempt—tells me a whole lot. It tells me that to her, my father has become a burden.

"His body is growing weaker," she says. "But his mind? As stubborn as ever."

"He is preparing himself," I say, in a cautious tone of voice. "Is he? Preparing himself—to die?"

"He is," she confirms.

And without having to ask, I instantly grasp what she fears— what I fear as well—what, at this point, is about to take place. My father is on his deathbed. He wishes to give his last word, which around here, is the equivalent of what you may call, a Last Will.

At stake are not just his physical assets, not just the fortune inherited from grandpa Abraham and later, amassed by my father, Isaac, over the course of a lifetime—but more than anything, his blessing. His vision for both Esav and me. He will foretell our future, even the survival of our descendants in generations to come. His words will be magical, everyone here knows that. Once uttered, these words can never be erased, nor can they be altered, and for certain, they will hold sway over our fate: The blessed son will become the master, the other one—a slave.

This is what is at stake here. The question of existence in history. The promise of success. My father wishes to give it, all of it, to his firstborn. And it makes no difference if I own the birthright, makes no difference to him.

The hunt is on. The meat Esav brings back from the hunt, that meat will become a love offering. In exchange, the old man will bless his chosen, his favorite child, the one he trusts.

And the birthright of the firstborn? What about that right? It is about to be trampled. Just my luck! Now that I have it, it has become worthless: No one cares anymore. The old man cares nothing for me. I will be left out. Left out in the cold.

"Come with me," says my mother. "We don't have much time."

I follow her behind the screen, to the deeper part of the tent. A dim light is streaming down, filtered coarsely through the canvas.

In the far corner, glimmering under a ray of light, stands her old chest. With a rusty creak, the lid comes open, revealing a secret compartment, out of which rises a long, hairy thing.

My mother gathers it softly into her arms, sinks her nails into it. Her eyes close and she takes a deep, sensual breath. Suddenly I recognize it: Her most treasured possession: The goatskin coat.

"And now," she says to herself out loud, "let the game begin!"

There is a ring of daring in her voice, as if she is bracing herself for a fight. Who is the enemy? Whom is she preparing to rip apart? I cannot tell. In her mind, this must be a power struggle. What is the prize, for her? Money? Power? Freedom?

At the tail of these questions, a thought crosses my mind: Can I trust her? Is she trying to manipulate me?

Still, come what may, I am with her. It suits me to be her partner, her partner even in crime. My mother counts on it. She thinks that for certain, she can control me. She must be relying on my gratitude in the years to come. Now for her, I recognize, this is a dangerous game. If I am not here, by her side, who will shield her from rage? Who will protect her from Esav?

"Sit down, dear," she tells me. "Let me measure you for size."

In a heartbeat, that unusually beautiful, striped shirt comes to mind. "Mom," I say plaintively. "This is no time for costumes —"

"Oh, but it is," says she, passing her fingers along my arm, rubbing me as if my skin is, somehow, too smooth, too sleek for the touch. Tortured by some vague sense of resentment, which I hate to call envy, I think about Esav. I cannot help but wonder if his arms, which look like a fleece, are more suitable for her taste.

"Hold out your arms," she tells me.

Then, in a blink of an eye, I see her throw the goatskin coat over my outstretched hands. That thing is spread out over me, weighing me down like a dead eagle.

"Wider," she says, and then, in a blink of an eye, it happens: That which up to this point, no one has expected—that which I have never thought possible—suddenly transpires before my eyes: Gripping the sleeve in one hand, the collar in the other one, my mother gives a harsh, vigorous pull. And with a sharp, ripping sound, the thing comes apart at the seam!

I am in utter disbelief. I am in tears. That which is dearest to her is now in shreds. So is my life. So is my family.

My mother is so focused that she has no time, and no inclination, it seems, to pay attention to my feelings. With a pleat sewn between her eyebrows, and quick, exact moves, she gives a pull here, a tug there until the torn sleeve, with its long, human-like hair, slides halfway over my hand and gets stuck, abruptly, on the elbow.

At that second it dawns on me—I understand, in its entirety, my mother's plan, which nearly brings me to split my sides and roar with laughter—but at a single hint from her, I hold it in. No need for other people to hear us.

Intoxicated, I marvel in her plan, and in my mind I shout: My God, this is so clever! So deceitful! This costume, I think, is so much fun! Designed for the pleasure, so to speak, of a blind man... Ha! What does he know! That damn blessing may yet be mine, after all.

In my excitement I stumble across a thought, which is so outlandish that immediately, it makes me sober up. "What if he suspects something," I ask, in a whisper. I hate to admit it, but it is not love for my father, nor respect for his age, that drive me to such hesitation. Rather, it is fear: The fear to be found out.

She lowers her eyes, thinking intensely, searching for an answer.

So I press on: "What if he touches me? He will guess, perhaps, that I am not the son I pretend to be. And so, instead of a blessing, I will end up, God forbid, being cursed!"

What can she say, I wonder. True, my mother is close to me. We could always think alike. But for the life of me, I cannot understand her right now. She is the mother of twins, so in my mind, she should love us both, in fairly equal measures. In the years to come I would often wonder: Why would a woman do this, why would she pit one son against another?

From the time of her wedding it took her, I am told, twenty years to conceive us. Twenty years of trying, desperately, to become pregnant, because in this place, and for this tribe, of what value is a childless woman?

So for a long time, she may have resented her social standing here. Her mind became pickled in its own juices, and she ended up being bitter inside, and so utterly devious. But I think, it is one thing for me to cheat my brother. It is another thing altogether, for her to do it to her son.

After a while, she stirs. Her hand hangs, for a moment, in midair, a motion designed to reach out to me, and hug me, perhaps, in her own manner. Yet I can see that it is only herself, in the end, that she embraces. "On me your sin," she smiles sweetly, placing a hand on her breast, where the heart can be found. "Let your curse be on me."

The sleeve, meanwhile, continues to climb, as if of its own accord, over my shoulder. By now it is covering the entire length of my arm. To my amazement, a part of me seems to have disappeared. Esav's arm is beginning to take shape in place of mine.

She leans over me and with a sharp eye, threads her needle. But for some reason, we cannot bear to look at each other eye to eye. "Give me one minute, let me mend it," she says, removed from me, smiling to herself. "We don't have much time, I'm afraid. Your brother is on the hunt, and so are we."

I sit there at her feet watching her work. My mother is so skillful in manipulating that sleeve. Inside of it, my limb feels hot, suffocated. I let her control me, control my hand. It is no longer my hand.

By and by, a perfect calm comes upon me. I have no thought in my head, no clue that this is to be the last sunrise, the last morning that I spend with my mother; no premonition that our time together is running out, and that I should kiss her, and hug her, and bid her farewell.

Yet for some reason, glancing around me, I commit to memory every aspect of this scene, every detail: The vivid pattern of the rug, spread across the dirt floor. The embroidered silk pillows, leaning against the woven headrest. The little blemish, barely visible in the corner of the blanket. The silver thread coming apart, at one point, at the bottom of the canvas. The jug of water, half hidden behind the curved leg of the bed.

I can hear little noises: The occasional cry of a newborn baby, searching blindly for his mother's breast. The light snores of the maidservants, some of whom are just starting to wake up, only to fall asleep again. The yawns of the shepherd boys, stretching their limbs lazily under the sheepskins in the neighboring tents. The unrest of the sheep, the lambs, the kids, the goats, all eager to go out there, to graze in the sun-flooded fields.

Meanwhile the needle flies back and forth, forth and back, over my shoulder, catching the light in its path. I am transfixed. I wish I could stay here forever. This place is so full of charms.

This hour is so intimate, so sweet, and it is fast coming to its bitter conclusion.

And the only thing that disturbs me, the only thing that stands here between us, is not being able to look each other in the eyes, during the last moments that remain to us.

My mother gets up. She is a petite woman, but the snakeskin shoes give her some stature. She throws the remains of the damaged coat back into the chest. Then she pulls out one of her fur hats and sinks her face into it, taking in the smell. "The air of the hunt," she says, then hands it to me. "Here, put it on."

After that, my mother attends to the cooking. I can hear the hiss, the slight hiss of the pot as it comes to a boil. I can smell the aroma. Somewhat bland to my taste—but then again, this is the way my father likes his meat. At any rate, he can barely swallow food nowadays.

She ladles a steaming hot portion onto a platter and sets it upon a large tray, so I can carry it over there, to his bedside. Then she gives me the slightest of hints. It is all set up. The time is now.

My arm covered with the hide of a kid, I stand up. Pretending to be that which I am not, I am ready, at long last, to do her bidding. Ready for my defining moment with my father: The old man is on his deathbed. He is waiting for me. Waiting there, in his tent, for his trusty, favorite son.

Chapter 3
A Favorite Son

For the third day in a row, one bird after another flew into my father's tent and tore into the canvas. On the first day, the maidservants mended the tear. On the second day they let it be, saying that in their opinion, the increased air circulation would do him some good, perhaps even revive him. And on the third day, at the sight of one open tear after another, a whisper spread around the camp, saying that this could be nothing else but an omen. It was on the fourth day that my mother decided to go in and see the old man.

By now she has sent away the maidservants, dismissed the guard and told me to stand near the entry, where the rope is double knotted over the peg of the tent, and prepare myself. I am itchy. The goatskin sleeve around my arm feels heavy and moist with sweat. It is as hairy as my twin brother Esav, perhaps even hairier.

"Look at that sleeve," she tells me. "It is not a costume. This is your skin. Feel it. Smell it. Say to yourself: My name is not Yankle. I am not me. I am bold, fierce, adventurous. I am my father's favorite son. I am Esav."

I fix the fur hat on my head, wipe the sweat off my upper lip and try to tell myself, over and over, that this arm is no longer mine. It is his. I am him. As such, this is to be my lucky day. It has started well: My brother has been out of the way all morning, hunting somewhere up there, in the mountains. Meanwhile, the stew for my father's meal has been dished into a plate and covered with a lid, ready to be carried in.

This is more than a meal. It is a token, a love offering from the son he loves. The chosen one. In exchange, the old man is to give his blessing, at which time his power will diminish. And the son, the one he loves, will take his place, and replace him as the head of the family, inheriting all his possessions.

The plot is ready, and my role, I repeat to myself, is well-rehearsed. Well, as well as can be. According to my mother, there is no time, and no need, really, for any more practice. Trying too hard, as you know, may be the best guaranty for failure.

"Your father is blind. Fool him," she says. "But do so, if you can, without resorting to lies."

To which I say, "How—"

"Don't you know?" she says, teasingly. "Think! What is the best, the most reliable way to deceive? It is this: Pay attention to what he needs, and then confirm that which he wants to believe, as if, Yankle, as if it were true."

She gathers her silk skirt, lifts it away from her high heel snakeskin shoes, and steps out of them. Right now she is about to enter the tent barefoot, as a proper show of respect for my father.

"Remember who you are," she whispers. "Now listen and learn."

I can hear her letting out a sigh.

"Oh, Isaac," she sighs. "What will I do without you?"

She must be extremely sorry to let him go, for her sadness seems as pressing and as urgent as her need for a proper will.

At first, my father is unmoved. "Oh, Becky," he says. "Don't start."

"Without you, I will be lost."

"Please, not that again."

Her voice trembles a little as she carries on, "Please, Isaac: What will become of me?"

"You have two sons—"

"Neither one of them will be here to help me, in my hour of need."

This gives him pause, after which he says, "What about that gift I gave you, long ago, that goatskin coat? Do you still have it?"

"Why," she says, and I know she is a bit startled. "But of course—"

"You never wear it. I was just wondering."

"It has a sleeve that needs mending."

"So then, in your hour of need, just put it on the auction block," he suggests, half-seriously. "It will fetch a small fortune!"

"Talking about a small fortune," she counters, "what about your little trunk, full of gold coins?"

"Being of a sound body and mind," he says, "I spent it all."

"On what, in heaven's name?"

"What! On what, Becky? Here I go, heaping all those bracelets, all those nose rings on one woman, and one woman alone, only to find out, in the end, the real extent of her gratitude!"

"Isaac my dear, you know well enough how grateful I am—"

"Becky my dear," he says, with a note of disdain. "What I know is this: Anyone else in my position would have at his disposal at least two or three legally registered wives, not to mention a respectably large harem, full of concubines—"

Being a practical woman, she decides to ignore that. "Fine, then," she says. "So now, dear: How about giving me some means of transportation? The rich women, I hear, those in the cities along the coast, in Ashdod and also in Ashkelon, they have started to buy new automobiles. And I, I live here in the desert but still, Isaac, I come from nobility, you know, from one of the richest families in the land."

"What kind of transportation?"

"A camel, for instance," she says. "Two humps, or more, as well as a driver or two, or more. And four leather saddles, the soft kind, of course. It would be but a small token, a token of prestige—"

"For goodness sake," he groans. "It's a camel you're talking about—not a Rolls Royce!"

"I see," she says. "You don't love me anymore."

For the first time in the conversation, his voice softens. "Don't cry, Becky," he pleads. "I love you. I will always love you—"

I imagine she must be smiling through the tears. "In that case," she says, "I will always take such good care of you."

"I am afraid," he admits to her, "of dying."

"Don't you worry. You will outlive us all."

"I am afraid," he says, "of leaving you."

To which she counters, "Can't get rid of me—not so fast, Isaac. You have a long life ahead of you. Everyone knows it! But one day," she adds, now in her playful manner, "I tell you, Isaac, one of these days I will make a complete fool out of you."

"I know it," he says, with a touch of sadness.

"Meanwhile," she says, with an entirely different tone, which is quite dry and seemingly resentful, "your son is here."

He understands instantly that which she has meant him to understand. "Esav?" he cries, with a voice so warm, so full of glee, that at once my heart starts to ache. "He's back, so soon?"

"Talk to him, dear, will you? He should treat me with respect, the way I deserve to be treated."

"I will tell him to do just that."

"He never listens to what I say," she complains. "Those girls he brings home every night, they make so much noise! I lie there in bed wide awake thinking, enough already! And the incense they burn, those shiksas, it gives out so much smoke—which is another reason why your eyesight, Isaac, is what it is."

"Let him come, Becky, let him in already."

I hear the slight rustle of her skirt, and her soft voice saying, "Wait, Isaac—" just before it becomes muffled. So sharply, so unexpectedly does it happen, that it makes me giddy with curiosity. And so, I do what I have to do: I lift the flap of the tent, allowing light in, to peek in on them, and what I see leaves me dumbfounded.

There she is, kneeling down before him amidst ripples of silk. She wraps her arms around his frail shoulders, draws closely and kisses him, long and full, on his mouth. And then, when she rises up, you can see that his face is confused, and his hand is trembling a little.

Presently my mother comes out, and steps into her shoes. She turns away from me   and pulls out a cute, embroidered handkerchief, which she uses now, to dry something in the corner of her eye. I find myself staring at her: if she, who is so cunning, so smart, is that susceptible, if, out of nowhere, she has fallen to emotion—then, what chance do I stand?

I have to wonder: what was that kiss? Her way to say farewell? Was it inspired by some old memory, some image of their younger days—or else, was it designed to make him vulnerable, make him ready for me, just in time for my entrance? I agonize, I puzzle over that kiss. Was it an act of love —or of deceit?

By now she has walked away. I cross the threshold. The flap falls shut behind me. And in an instant, a change comes upon me. I am deceit. I become the son he wants me to be. His favorite son.

The old man calls my name, and I advance in the darkness in the direction of his voice, bumping against a shelf here, a bench there. First, near the entrance, I touch the cold surface of an hourglass, nearly tipping it over. A leather scroll drops down accidentally and spreads across my path. Meanwhile the wind is flapping, slapping across the canvas, a bird comes squawking overhead, and with every step I can hear a sound that is even higher than all that: my heart, racing wildly.

At last I reach his bed, above which I can see two open tears in the canvas. Slanting down from there are two long rays, the rays of morning light, the glare of which beams down directly upon his eyes, his odd, blind eyes.

The eyelids are so fine, the little veins so delicate, so transparent, that in a flash I begin to worry. Can I fool him—or am I making a fool of myself? Can he see, even vaguely? Can he tell, somehow, who I am, perhaps by the slightness of my frame, or the general shape of my shoulders?

Naturally, I have to test it. So I raise my Esav arm, the one with the hairy sleeve. I raise it with the thought of bringing it down upon him in one fell swoop, right next to his cheek, and stopping just short of a slap. Would he flinch? Would he give a flutter? My hand flies up. I freeze. But then, an incredible thing happens. You would not believe it—I do not believe it myself! I cannot, for the life of me, control it any further.

At first I figure that the old man must have cast some spell over me. By all accounts, he is a master of scriptures and can recite magical chants in a number of ancient languages. I stand there, with my arm frozen in the air over him, and with my eyes burning in their sockets as if to drill a hole in him. But nothing seems to have changed: he does not squirm, nor does he stir under my gaze. And so, little by little, I grow calmer.

My muscles start to relax and then, of its own accord, my limb comes down to rest at my side. I lay a hand on him and, quite casually, brush against his skin to make sure he feels me.

"Esav," he says. "My dear child."

I come close and, quite unlike me, give him a hug. To my surprise, it feels good. He is much smaller than I have expected, less formidable, too. And so, there is no point right now in my usual rebellion. His fingers lift from the blanket. They hang in midair, as though they can sense me, somehow, without even touching. Then he strokes the hair on my goatskin sleeve.

A big sigh rises from my heart. I nearly let it fly from my lips —but hold back just in time. Blind men, so I heard, can develop an acute sense of hearing, to compensate for the loss of their eyesight. Therefore, I know I should not talk. On the other hand, I should not be completely silent.

Now, that is unfortunate. Silence, especially the spiteful kind, is something I understand. I have used it often, in my lifelong fight against him. But now, it would not do, because in this conversation, the last one, I have to be not only present, but engaged. So, in place of greeting my father, I do what by instinct I know he may expect to hear: I let out a cough.

The old man tries to pull up his body, then sinks back into his pillows.

"You must be heartbroken," he says, "to see me like this."

I cough again.

"Just close your eyes," says my father. "Remember me as I was, and in return, I will tell you what your fortune will be."

How can he do that, I ask you, when he does not even have a clue who I am?

He strokes my fur hat and says, "Ah! The air of the hunt! How I love that about you! So rarely have I set foot outside the camp. How I envy you! How I wish you could take me along, out there to the faraway mountains, to see you chase the wild beast!"

I sit down on his bed with a heaviest thud I can make, and he says, "My big, strong boy! So now, you tell me: how can a hunter become a healer?"

I have no patience for his strange riddles, and so I shrug.

"You will have to find a way," he says, to himself this time. "Yes, you will. I am quite certain. Between my two sons, it must be you."

"Aha," I say, wishing he would hurry up already and bless me, whoever the hell I am.

"Someday," he predicts, "my descendants will swear by the name of God, the God of Abraham, the God of Isaac and the God of Esav!"

"Aha."

"Yes," he insists again, as if to convince himself, "It must be you. Come on now, let me smell that stew."

I place the tray at his bedside, lift the lid off the plate and prepare to feed the old man, at which time he sits up and says, "No! What are you doing?"

I step back, stunned to learn that already I must have made a mistake.

He pleats his forehead and at once, falls to silence, a tense, hard silence which I dare not break, for fear of being recognized.

After a while he makes himself relax, and says to me, "Eat, Esav. Go on, my child, I know you must be hungry."

I dare not say Aha this time—but all of a sudden I understand the game: I understand the role which my brother has been playing lately. The old man can barely swallow food anymore. Instead, it has been Esav who licks his plate clean for him.

No one knows this, not even my mother! Clearly, it helps everyone believe that old Isaac, the head of our little clan is still healthy, still strong enough and capable to lead, and it helps my brother, no doubt, into a double helping every single meal.

I know what has to be done. So I dip the spoon into the stew, and raise it to my lips—but I cannot bring myself to take a bite, not so much because it is too bland—but rather, because my throat is too damn dry. I am too anxious, too uptight, really. So instead, I make a loud swallowing sound which, luckily, satisfies my father, because he leans back, spreads open his thin arms and gives me a big smile.

"Now, you may not realize it," he says to me, "but Yankle and I, we are very much alike."

My heart skips a beat at the mention of my real name, which forces me to cough up, "How?"

To which he says, "I love Yankle. Love him more than he knows, more that he can ever imagine. I am a dreamer. So is he. Both of us like to stay within the confines of the tent. It is a sheltered existence that we have both lead."

I make a swallowing sound, and he goes on.

"I am afraid that the future of this family, its survival in this harsh, treacherous land, cannot be entrusted into the hands of someone who, until now, has never been out and about. Never explored a new path. Never been tested by the elements."

I hate him for what he has just said, because I know, deep in my heart, that there is truth in it.

"In all things," he goes on, "Yankle follows his mother. So you tell me: how can a follower become a leader?"

I have to swallow that, too—but feel it is unfair. Whatever. Why should I even bother with his stupid riddles? My character, I figure, is entirely the old man's fault! He was the one to name me Yankle, which in Hebrew means 'a follower,' for no better reason than the fact I was born second, a split second after my twin brother. How can you blame me for that?

Whatever! I hate that name. Hate my identity. I hate me. Hate my father for naming me—naming me for my weakness, right there at birth.

Now, all of a sudden, he wants me to change? A little too late for that!

"May God help me," he whispers. "May He help us all, if I choose wrong!"

Oh, God again! I hate him for his faith, hate him for his doubts, too.

I note the slightly labored breath with which he utters his words. "I have come to the conclusion," he says, "based on many, many years of experience, that I can expect with perfect certainty, that my advice will be utterly and immediately ignored."

Amen to that, I say to myself. But at the same time, I can sense that my fury is waning, that it has left me already. And listening to him, listening to how he inhales and exhales with such difficulty, I start to feel sorry for him.

Despite his weakness, his voice rises, for a moment, to a boom. "I am the son of Abraham. It was for a life of sacrifice that I was chosen. You can take it from me: beware, my son! Being the favorite son is as much of a curse as being the one rejected."

From then on I find myself leaning closer and closer, just so I can hear him. My Esav arm hangs on my Yankle frame just as heavily as before—but somehow I am no longer split between my parts. A great sense of loss comes over me, body and soul, entire.

Without even looking at the entrance to the tent, without even touching the cold surface of the hourglass, I know: it is nearly empty. The sand is running out. For us, there is no more time. He will never realize who it was standing there by his bedside, overcome and awash with tears.

I let one word escape, hoping that he cannot catch the sound of it—but wishing, in spite of myself, that he would.

"Dad," I whisper.

It is then that he raises his hand and with a strength I did not know he possessed, takes hold of my limb. He runs his fingers through the hair of the goatskin sleeve, comes as high up as my heart—and then, loses his breath and lets go. "The arm is the arm of Esav," he whispers. "But the voice is the voice of Yankle."

He falls silent, and I wait. I am beside myself with worry: in his mind, who am I? There is no way to tell. He would not reveal it, except to say, at last, "Now, what I am about to tell you, son, will guide you and protect you in the future," after which he tells me that which I came here to hear: I shall become my brother's master, he—my slave.

This, I know, is a crucial sentence. From this moment on it can never be undone, not even by my father, no matter how pathetically my brother will shed tears, or how intensely he will plead with him.

My father follows it with a long list of advice. His words are not only strange—but in one case, entirely new to me. In halting sentences he tries to explain that which to him, is inexplicable, and to me—plain hard to grasp. Something about finding a connection to something abstract, without face or name. He asks me about something higher, greater than myself?

Meanwhile I start to count time. Time is a fearsome thing, especially when you are expecting your brother. He will be back any moment now, to claim that which is his, which is his to lose: this blessing.

I listen to sounds from outside: birds come flapping their wings over us in a feverish flutter. I look up at the two open tears in the canvas overhead, and know that by now, it must be high noon.

I know it because the two rays of light have changed direction by now: they fall straight down like heavy ropes, like a ladder, really, with no degree of slanting.

I try to focus on my dad, and then, in a blink of an eye, it happens: things go dark before my eyes and right there, for the first time in my life, I think I see angels, climbing down that ladder, kissing his feet, which are nearly white, and then flying away.

I wipe my eyes in amazement, only to realize it was nothing, nothing but an odd, fleeting vision. And yet, I wonder.

Earlier in the day, I expected to obtain great riches from the old man, and now I have come to realize that what I possess now—what I have just taken from my dad—is a fortune beyond my imagination. The fortune of a dreamer: to be connected, if only for a second, to something higher and greater than myself, something vast and eternal. A ladder of sorts. A ladder to heaven.

I bend my head before him. He holds me. It is with great difficulty that he utters, "Forgive me, son, if I have hurt you." His lips move again, and I believe they are forming the words, "I forgive—"

He is in agony. I turn my head away from him, and the first thing I see, on the outer side of the tent—just below the flap—is my mother's high heel, snakeskin shoes. They are pacing nervously to and fro, between one peg and another. I figure she is there to warn me. Perhaps she wonders what is being said. From time to time the shoes come to a stop, and you can see a shape being pressed to the canvas: her ear, listening in, hearing nothing, because at this point, the only sound to be heard is coming from outside.

From the far edge of the camp there rises a loud, terrible roar, full of rage. At first I wonder what beast could have uttered this cry—but soon I realize it could be only one: my brother. I understand his pain. He is no longer the favorite son. His luck has turned, and he knows it.

As for me—I am so lucky that, for fear of being murdered by him, I have to run. So I do what comes naturally, and what I will come to regret one day: I turn my back on my dad. I tell myself that I have to leave him lying here, fighting for his breath. Time is up. Have to go.

And so, I release myself from his grip and rise up, rise away, for the first time, with a new, unfamiliar feeling in my heart. This, I think, is a fresh beginning.

My name is Yankle. I am blessed.

Chapter 4
The Curse of the Striped Shirt

Y ou may have heard those rumors about me: how I escaped by moonlight, how I hid inside each one of the seven wells of Beersheba, with nothing in my possession but the shirt on my back, how I eluded my enemy, my brother, and then, how frightened I was, how alone. I'm afraid you have been, at best, misinformed—or, more probably, misled by some romantic foolery, some fiction and lies, the kind of which can easily be found, and in abundance I might add, in the holy scriptures.

I insist: it was not moonlight but rather, high noon. I was wearing no shirt whatsoever—nothing, really, but a goatskin sleeve. There was only one well in which I could hide, not seven. And most importantly, I was hardly alone, for the entire camp— all the maidservants, the shepherds, the guards—stood aghast all around me. So now, you must see that I could not, despite my best intentions, escape stealthily out of there, nor could I elude anyone.

Instead I was flung out, kicking and screaming, with tugs and pulls loosening the remaining shreds of my clothes, and whacks and smacks coming at my bare back from all directions. My left eye swelled up to such a degree that out of necessity, I resorted to use the right one—only to discover, once I raised my head from the dirt, that my brother was standing right over me. His foot could be seen coming straight at me, at an easygoing, unhurried pace, until it turned into a full blown kick.

I managed to roll away, mainly by flailing my arms wildly over my head. With a great sense of urgency I crawled on all four through the crowd, and hid inside the closest well. Luckily it was bone dry, thanks to a yearlong drought. And so for a second, I could hang there by my fingernails and pant, and catch my breath. Then I tiptoed behind the corner, right into the shade of my mother's tent.

From there I took a plunge and hurled myself downhill—where, to my utter disappointment, I found out that my brother had already caught up to where I was headed, and was waiting there for me with open arms. He made a point of letting me know that his hate for me would, by no means, stand in the way of our closeness.

"Come, Yankle," said Esav. "I promise not to hurt you."

"Really," I said. "Can I trust you?"

"Aha," said he. "I will just kill you."

His bulging, bloodshot eyes were full of vigor, and so, unfortunately, was his fist. It met my chin once, then again, attempting to drive the point home, but on the third try, he missed—which was the sole reason why I still had my wits about me.

I staggered away, aided in my movement by the quaking of my knees. A desire to live made me, somehow, light on my feet. I turned and ran, leaving my brother behind, way back in the dust. I could no longer see him. He may have given up the chase —but still, knowing his skill as a hunter, I had to keep on going, opening a measure of distance between us. An hour later I found myself crossing the dry river bed, which was such a long distance from camp, so far from where I used to feel safe, that it was, for me, an unknown, dangerous zone.

The sun scorched overhead, beating upon the steep, rocky slopes. I hesitated. I looked back. The peaks of the tents had shrunk away. A short time later, they disappeared completely from view.

The notion of asking my brother—no, begging him—to forgive me, crossed my mind. I thought of retracing my footprints and perhaps, finding my way back home, only to realize, by nightfall, that those footprints had led me astray.

I must have been walking around in circles that entire day, which made me feel helpless. I thought that in the future, if I was lucky enough to have one, I could never become more helpless than this. How wrong was I then!

Now I laid down under some wilted bushes, using a rock for a pillow. So miserably disgraced, so alone was I, that I wished to bury myself right there in the sand. A great blackness yawned upon me. It was like no other night sky I had ever seen before.

Back home, I remembered, it would be lit up by the campfire, around which the family would gather for the evening meal. The faces of the young girls, sitting with their skirts spread on the woven mat, would blush. You could see their cheeks flaming as they giggled, hinting at the shepherds, who would rise up then, stand in a loop and play their flutes, made out of reeds, or strum their stringed instruments, made out of sheep sinews.

The blaze of the fire would be mirrored in my father's eyes, and looking at him, you could barely believe he was going blind. His rich voice would lead us in songs, which turned, gradually, into wordless melodies, as the wine cask was passed from one hand to another, making its way several times around the fire.

At bedtime you could spot, through the canvas of your tent, the glitter of my mother's candlelight. Her soft, charming voice would bid goodnight to you, goodnight to all.

Then, from the maidservant's quarters, you could hear the gurgle of a baby, falling asleep on his mother's breast. And later, the whispers of love making from one tent, then another, followed by peaceful rhythms of breathing. All around you, men and women stirring, from time to time, in their sleep.

The glow of this memory was as tempting and as fanciful as delusion. I ached for warmth, and wished I could leap, somehow, over time and distance, and find my way back into that circle. I wished I could sit there by the fire pit, and stretch out my hands, even blacken them by touching the dying embers.

Now in this place, the moonless sky was completely devoid of light, and for the first time in my life I was forced to listen, really listen, to the desert.

Here was the void. The silence of God.

I was trying desperately to separate it into notes, invent some variants, some life. I imagined I could hear a rustling in the dry, brittle brush.

Could roaches be creeping over me? Could a scorpion be slithering under my rock? I sat up, my mind tortured by things of phantasy, such as the noiseless flight of vultures. But then I decided to calm my nerves. I yelled, Come! Flap your wings! Let me hear you! Come here, scavengers, prey upon me! Pick my bones! Then the echo answered, "Bones, bones..."

Let them perch on me, upon my skull! Who cares? Come morning, my brother would find me. He would spill tears all over my remains. For my untimely death, he would surely blame himself. My mother, too, would sob. She would grieve inconsolably. Now that ought to teach them, teach them all a big lesson!

There was a chill in the air. It quivered with the last echoes of the echoes of my voice. And then—I swear, this is no exaggeration—the heavens opened up right there, before my eyes.

This must be a dream, I said to myself. A dream born out of exhaustion. A vision, which I had seen once before, one that would keep coming back to me in later years, even in my old age —even as late as tonight!

Nowadays, however, I am so much wiser, so much more cautious. Hush! Don't tell my sons. Are they here? Let them not hear that which I am about to tell you, because I know, all too well, what happens to old men, crazy old men who are nearly blind, but can see things, things that no other human can see.

But I digress. A distant lightning tore through the sky, and in a flash, I thought I saw a ladder. It was set up on earth, and the top of it reached to heaven, turning from time to time, like a flame in the wind. And behold! Winged creatures were ascending and descending on it. Were they lost souls, rising up from skeletons in the desert, and coming down to mourn them?

Or else, were they angels, pulling my soul up, in agony and distress—and then, seeing how weak, how famished I was, coming back to hold me, in pity and compassion?

The sight vanished in smoke, and I wiped my eyes in amazement.

Soon I fell asleep, and dreamt of the long way awaiting me, and of the years of exile lying ahead, in foreign places, places faraway from home, and I saw myself coming back one day, with sons and daughters, and their sons and their daughters, a family, a tribe, a people, a multitude like the dust of the earth.

And from the dust of the earth I awoke, to a clap of thunder. I knew instantly what it meant: the dry spell had broken! In a matter of minutes, the crevices and cracks around me filled up. They were bubbling with water.

Rain washed over me, lightly at first. I opened my mouth and let it trickle in, let it break my thirst. I drank it up, in big, long gulps. I was intoxicated! I was alive! I sprang to my feet and it was just then that I saw, coming out of nowhere, a river gushing, rushing into the valley.

I had heard of flash flooding before—but never did I stand in the midst of it. I started up the slope. My path was slippery, for a torrent of rain poured down mercilessly upon the earth. At one point I stopped to try and catch my breath. Was it my imagination? Between one thunder clap and another, I could hear a sound, a delicate clip clop coming towards me from the top of the mountain.

And look: out there in the damp distance, against the backdrop of a clouded sunrise, you could detect two humps traveling in unison along the ridge. In a little bit, a camel came into view. And up there in the saddle, riding like a queen, wrapped in her goatskin coat, was no other than the woman I admired, the woman I adored: my mother.

Hope filled my heart. She was my shelter, my home! With her, I knew I would be safe, safe from hunger, safe from thirst, and above all, safe from my brother. With a new burst of energy, I scrambled over the last few boulders that stood between us, and cried out for her.

The clip clop came to a stop. I drew closer, so close that by now, those long eyelashes and those ear hairs, used by the camel as a barrier against sand, swung by and gave my nose a sudden tickle. Meanwhile, my mother's face remained high above me, curiously out of sight, hidden behind a black veil. And so, it was only by her shoes, which hung right there at eye-level, that you could recognize her.

"Mom!" I cried.

She gave no answer.

"Mom!" I cried, even louder this time. "Help! Please, help me!"

To which she whispered, "Hush, my child."

I shrank back. Long seconds passed, during which rain kept coming, sheets and sheets of rain. Her veil was so soaked—it clung so tightly to the features of her face—that by now, I could begin to guess her expression, even the movements of her eyes.

Her gaze, I noticed, flew far beyond me. It seemed to focus at something—someone—in the direction from where I had come last night. Somehow I knew who it was, even before turning around.

Right there, on the opposite hill, he stepped forth, his arrow slung into his bow. My brother raised it slowly, aimed directly at my heart, and drew the bow, but at the critical second he halted, stopping just short of releasing the string. His hand seemed to waver, and just as I allowed myself to breathe more freely, I caught him taking one more step. This time he pointed the arrow higher, aiming it at her—at our mother. For what seemed like an eternity, the three of us froze in position.

She stuck up her chin, looking at him steadily, even defiantly. I closed my eyes. The only sound that could be heard was water, filling up the deep divide between us and him.

When I opened my eyes, my brother was gone. It was then that her bold expression gave way to tears. She started laughing, a wild laughter mixed with cries. In a fit of rage, she shed her snakeskin shoes and threw them, one high heel shoe after another, in his direction. And one after another they splashed into the water and sank in. I figured, good riddance. Those shoes were ill-suited, anyway, for the desert sand.

"What did I do," cried my mother, "to deserve this?"

She sounded so pure, so innocent, that if I did not know any better, I would swear that this woman was incapable of any sort of manipulation.

No, she could not possibly have crafted the best, the most reliable way to deceive her husband. She could not have plotted against her son. Her tone was so injured as to convince not only me, but herself as well. It would be easier to believe that I had gone mad, that my grasp on reality must have failed me, that truth had no basis in facts.

She moaned, "Where did I go wrong?"

How could I answer? I might as well have asked that question myself. Like a good, faithful son, I had followed her instructions, followed them to the letter, and took advantage of my old man, so that in his blindness, he had given me that which belonged to my brother, that which I did not deserve: the last blessing.

Well, if that was a blessing, I wonder what a curse might look like, because here I was, lost, hungry, empty-handed, and stranded in the middle of nowhere. Where, I ask you, did I go wrong? It was all her fault! Her calculations had missed the mark and brought me here, to this place. Perhaps she figured that once Isaac blessed me, Esav would realize who was really the one in power, and in time, he would bring himself to bow down before her.

Despite this minor mistake on her part I trusted that she, of all people, could show me the way out. My mother was such a shrewd woman, a woman unlike any other. Perhaps she could read my mind.

"I am not like other women, never was," she said. "During the first years of marriage I was incapable of giving life. I am no goddess of fertility, you know. So for twenty years I bathed in holy water. For twenty years I prayed on my knees for children, and in the end, all that effort did pay off: I was pregnant! Not one baby, but twins! Oh, the bliss, the happiness! Right from the start they kicked me, on the double. First he, then you, you, he. Both of you kicked so hard I would fold over..."

Right away I felt defeated by the endless suffering, which she professed to have experienced on my behalf. My God, she was the mother of all Jewish Mothers! She was such an expert at guilt! You had to admire her.

"I nearly died at childbirth," she whispered. "Oh God, I wish I did."

I wanted to hug her, to calm her down, but she was perched up there, way out of reach.

"Did I not feed both of you, hold you when you were sick, teach you everything you know?" said my mother. "What, in God's name, did I do to deserve this?"

"What did I do?" said I.

To which she replied, "This is about me, not you."

I looked at her black veil and it dawned on me, suddenly, that she was in mourning, and that in my absence, my father, Isaac, had passed away.

"I wish I were dead," she said, and then her hand fell, sleeveless, out of that coat.

I had been wondering why she was wearing it—her pristine, expensive goatskin coat—which by now, looked utterly disheveled.

It looked rumpled not only because she had ripped out that sleeve, not only because it was soaked wet, and not only because its hair, that fine, long, humanlike hair, was curled out of shape, but mainly because her arm, coming out of that hole where the sleeve used to be, looked bare, almost mangled.

That missing sleeve which I was now wearing on my own arm, was the evidence linking us together. That sleeve, to me, was more than a costume. It was part of a plot, and she was my partner, my partner even in crime. Her finger trembled slightly as she pointed back, vaguely in the direction of the camp.

"They forced me to wear the coat," she told me. "When Isaac died, they sneered at me. They said, Wear it. It's your mantle of shame."

"Forget them," I said. "I love you. Now, you are both my mother and my father."

At the sound of my words she bent over and kissed me on my forehead, which made me gush on, "Come with me! I know I don't know where I am going, you know, but wherever it is, Mom, I promise: you'll be safe with me!"

"You?" she said, chuckling to herself. "Ha! If I put you in a brown paper bag, I bet you would never, I mean not ever, find your way out!"

That really stung. The other day, I recalled, my father had asked me, How could a follower become a leader? It was too late to go back to him, too late to answer. But now I swore, I promised myself: I would learn to live by my wits, even in the harshest of conditions. Even here in the desert. I would find water to drink, even if I had to suck it out of a rock with my cracked lips. I would find food, even if I had to skin wildcats and scorpions with my bare fingers. I would survive, even if it had to kill me. Never again will she—or he, or anyone—ridicule me!

Still chuckling, my mother thrust a little bundle, tied in a knot, into my hands. With that, she gave a slight nudge to the camel, turned it swiftly around and with a clip and a clop away she went, taking her chances elsewhere, into a rainy fog.

Never again would I see her. Upon my return to this place, more than two decades later, I would learn that my brother never forgave her for loving me, loving me only, and in the end, her funeral was poorly attended, because the letter announcing her death was never delivered to me. And no wonder. He could not bring himself to write it, nor did he come there himself to lay her to rest.

Again, I digress. Back to the matter at hand. I untied the knot, opened the little bundle she had just given me, and what do you think I found inside? Food? Drink? A map, perhaps, to guide me on my way? No, no and no!

It had a hint of her jasmine perfume, and when I unfolded the thing, I recognized the pattern of the weave. It was her shirt, that unusually beautiful shirt, striped blue-on-white, the same one she had let me try on, way back in the past, when I was a little child.

It was a token of her love for me, her love only for me. I caressed the fabric, fondled it between my fingers. It gave a soft swoosh, above which I could hear, as vividly as I hear you, the resonant, deep voice of my father.

"Beware, my son!" said the voice. "Being the favorite son is as much of a curse as being the one rejected."

My heart sank and at once, I knew I should bury that shirt. He who wore it would forever be cursed. But I could not bring myself to do it.

It was, after all, the only thing I had, the only thing to which I could cling, a small reminder of home, of love, of my mother. So instead, I made myself a solemn promise: this curse stops here, with me. I would never pass it on to my children, neither would I single out one of them from the rest, to make him my favorite.

I have no clue why you laugh, but I can tell by the sound of it, how bitter you must be, perhaps even resentful. What a pity, son! Up to now you have been listening so patiently. Was it something I said? I guess you have heard this story already. Maybe you have heard it many, many times before. Forgive an old man. What did you say your name was? Forgive me, these days I have no memory for names anymore.

In the years to come, I came to father many sons. They are flesh of my flesh. So they tell me. Blood of my blood. Yet somehow I can barely remember their names. One of these days, I tell you, they would try to fool me, like I did my own father. I guess it is the nature of things. Which is why I keep telling myself, Beware. Watch out. Eye each and every one of them with great suspicion.

I like to think of myself as a modern man. A confused one. One left to his own devices, because of one thing: the silence of God. When Isaac, my father, lay on his deathbed, waiting for me, or rather, for his favorite son to come in, he suspected, somehow, that he was about to be fooled. And yet, God kept silent. Now, all these years later, I wonder about it.

God did not help the old man. He gave no warning to him, not one whisper in his ear, not a single clue. Now as then, He is utterly still, and will not alert me when my time comes, when they, my sons, flesh of my flesh, blood of my blood, are ready to face me, to fool their old man.

As I said, I could not care less for any of them—until, that is, Yoseph. Yosele my son, my son, Yosele.

When he was born—were you here, then? Did you see him? Really! So cute, so handsome!—I forgot that curse, the curse of being the favorite one. Even worse, I forgot the promise I made to myself, never to pass it on. And so I wrapped him tightly, with all my hope, all my love, all my yearning, wrapped him in that beautifully striped shirt, paying no attention—none whatsoever —to the jealousy flashing, every now and again, from the eyes of his brothers.

What is it with you? Why are you shuffling around so much, on that bench? Are you uncomfortable? No? Then I must be boring you. I admit, I can be overbearing at times. Forgive me. Why I go on and on like that, I have no idea.

You wanted to say something? Who are you? Reuben? I do not know you, do I? You are my child, you say? My firstborn? Flesh of my flesh, blood of my blood? Forgive an old man. I do not know you.

No need to cry. I do not remember, is all.

You are in my way. I cannot see. Right there, behind you is that light, that ladder to heaven, and behold: an angel is starting to drift away slowly, slowly fading away, just like smoke... Can you see it? No? There, in all its glory, is the silence of God. I must watch. I must learn to accept it. Now, can you move? The other way, if you don't mind. And remember, don't tell my sons, please don't tell anyone I said this.

Now where is my sweet child, my Yosele? Late, I'm afraid, so very late. He did not come home last night. I waited. I waited past midnight. By the crack of dawn, I fell to dreaming. I thought I heard a scream for help, a terrifying, bone-chilling scream. Did you hear it, too? No? How strange. Morning came and went, then noon, then evening—and nothing. Still, no sign of him. Listen... Can you hear a voice? Is he calling my name?

My heart, this foolish old heart, is heavy. There is a voice, I trust, a voice calling me out there. It is so faint, so high pitched that perhaps no one but me can hear it. Maybe it is nothing, nothing but the desert wind, shrieking. Sometimes, if you listen hard, it can sound like a tortured soul. Yes, it is the wind all right. It must be. I have to believe it, I do, really. If he comes back, don't tell him I said any of this.

It is the end of the day, and my eyes are so weak. I cover them with my wrinkled hands. They look like my father's. In their flesh I can see a web of blood vessels. It is a strange sight. Is this my body? Or am I beginning, perhaps, to lose my mind?

I try to recover. Gradually I become more alert and—bracing myself—I can hear things with great clarity. First, the silence. So dead, so complete. So divine, even. Then, you. You moving, you taking something out of that bundle, something I do not wish to see. It gives a slight, subtle swoosh... You are holding it in your hands, raising it to my eyes, asking me some question, over and again until, in my despair, I have no choice. I stamp my foot, trying not to hear, not to look. I am beside myself, so desperate to stop you. At last I cry, Enough!

Oh please... Just stop... There is no need to ask me anymore, do I recognize this thing—this unusually beautiful, striped thing that is slashed here, and here it is torn to pieces... And even before I can smell the blood—even before I can feel the rips in that which was his shirt—I hear someone wailing, roaring like a wild animal, like a father, in agony, in pain, from the depth of my soul.

Let me be. I grieve alone. I have no family. You are no blood of mine. Now go. Go away, son.

~ The End ~

About the Cover

The cover of this book is based on a mixed media painting I painted not long ago. In it I floated various paints on the paper, letting them drizzle and mix, to create an intricate, fiery flow of color. Then when they dried out I came in with a black pen, and drew just a few lines to suggest the figure.

To me, this is what this image means: looking directly at yourself, facing the pain and the ugly imperfections within, without any attempt to mask who you are—even if you find yourself on the verge of a meltdown. Which is the process the protagonist, Yankle, is going through in this story. He finds himself coming to terms with his core being, with how the tension between his emotions and needs has driven him over a lifetime.

As in my previous book cover designs, the glyphs of the book title and the author name cast subtle shadows over the image. However, one thing is different here: two of the glyphs (the 'U' and the 'P') of the author name cast a shadow like all the other letters, but they themselves—the objects that cast the shadows—are intentionally missing. Why? For two reasons:

First, because often in my art I discover that the eye is drawn to the unexpected, and the brain craves a riddle, a missing link to resolve. The observer, then, becomes highly engaged with the art, and in a sense—by working to bring it to completion—

becomes its creator. And second, because this missing link is a symbol, an indication of the flawed character in this story.

About This Book

This story is a present-day twist on the biblical story of Jacob and his mother Rebecca plotting together against the elderly father Isaac, who is lying on his deathbed, in order to get their hands on the inheritance, and on the power in the family. This is no old fairy tale. Its power is here and now, in each one of us.

Listening to Yankle telling his take on events, we understand the bitter rivalry between him and his brother. We become intimately engaged with every detail of the plot, and every shade of emotion in these flawed, yet fascinating characters. He yearns to become his father's favorite son, seeing only one way open to him: deceit.

In planning his deception, it is not love for his father, nor respect for his age that drives his hesitation--rather, it is the fear to be found out. And so--covering his arm with the hide of a kid, pretending to be that which he is not--he is now ready for the last moment he is going to have with his father.

This is so much more than a morality tale. Do you find sibling rivalry in adults intriguing? Are you troubled by the notion that the sins of the fathers will be visited upon the children? If so, you will find this story utterly captivating.

About the Author

U vi Poznansky is a *USA TODAY* bestselling, award-winning author, poet and artist. "I paint with my pen," she says, "and write with my paintbrush."

Uvi earned her B. A. in Architecture and Town Planning from the Technion in Haifa, Israel. During her studies and in the years immediately following her graduation, she practiced with an innovative Architectural firm, taking part in the design of a large-scale project, *Home for the Soldier*.

Having moved to Troy, N.Y. with her husband and two children, Uvi received a Fellowship grant and a Teaching Assistantship from the Architecture department at Rensselaer Polytechnic Institute. There, she guided teams in a variety of design projects and earned her M.A. in Architecture. Then, taking a sharp turn in her education, she earned her M.S. degree in Computer Science from the University of Michigan.

During the years she spent in advancing her career—first as an architect, and later as a software engineer, software team leader, software manager and a software consultant (with an emphasis on user interface for medical instruments devices)— she wrote and painted constantly. In addition, she taught art appreciation classes.

Her versatile body of work can be seen in two websites: her blog includes thoughts about the creative process, reader reviews, author interviews, excerpts from her novels, voice clips from her audiobooks, poems and short stories. Her art site includes bronze and ceramic sculptures, paper engineering projects, oil and watercolor paintings, charcoal, pen and pencil drawings, and mixed media.

Coma Confidential, Overkill, Overdose, and Overdue are novels in the *Ash Suspense Thrillers with a Dash of Romance* series. With each new case, Ash uses grit and intuition to solve the crime.

Virtually Lace is the first volume in a multi-author thriller series, *High-Tech Crime Solvers*, where the authors bring each other's characters into their books.

My Own Voice, The White Piano, The Music of Us, Dancing with Air, and *Marriage before Death* are novels in the *Still Life with Memories* series, a family saga with a love story that develops in the face of hardship and illness over two generations, starting at the 1980's, then harkening back to WWII when Lenny, a soldier, and Natasha, a rising star, first met. These books are also offered in two bundles: *Apart from Love* and *Apart from War.*

Rise to Power, A Peek at Bathsheba, and *The Edge of Revolt* are novels in *The David Chronicles,* telling the story of David as you have never heard it before: from the king himself, telling the unofficial version, the one he never allowed his court scribes to recount. In his mind, history is written to praise the victorious— but at the last stretch of his illustrious life, he feels an irresistible urge to tell the truth. These books are also offered in a trilogy.

In addition, *The David Chronicles* includes six art collections: *Inspired by Art: Fighting Goliath, Inspired by Art: Fall of a Giant, Inspired by Art: Rise to Power, Inspired by Art: A Peek at Bathsheba, Inspired by Art: The Edge of Revolt,* and *Inspired by Art: The Last Concubine.*

A Favorite Son, a new-age twist on an old yarn, is inspired by the biblical story of Jacob and his mother Rebecca, plotting together against the elderly father Isaac, who is lying on his deathbed.

Twisted is a unique collection, laden with shades of mystery. Here, you will come into a dark, strange world, a hyper-reality where nearly everything is firmly rooted in the familiar— except for some quirky detail that twists the yarn.

Home and *Can We Still Love*, Uvi's deeply moving poetry books in tribute of her father, include her poetry and prose as well as translated poems from the pen of her father, the poet, author and artist Zeev Kachel.

Uvi wrote and illustrated two children's books, *Jess and Wiggle* and *Now I Am Paper*. Watch the beautiful animations she created for these books on YouTube.

A Note to the Reader

Thank you for reading this book! I hope you enjoyed it. If you did, I invite you to check out more books from the same pen. There is always a new project on my drawing board, so come back to check it out.

I would love to hear what you thought of this book. You have the power of bringing it to the attention of more readers, by posting your own review. It would mean so much to me.

And another thing you can do to help me spread the word is this: please tell your friends about my work. How else will they hear about the story? How else will the characters, who sprang from my mind onto these pages, leap from there into new minds?

Bonus Excerpts
Excerpt: A Peek at Bathsheba

Wrapped in a long, flowing fabric that creates countless folds around her curves, she loosens just the top of it and lets it slide off her head—only to reveal a blush, and mischievous glint, shining in her eye. It is over that sparkle that I catch a sudden reflection, coming from the back window, of a full moon.

Looking left, right, and down the staircase, to make sure no one is lurking outside my chamber door, I let her in. Then I lock it behind her, so no one may intrude upon us.

In a manner of greeting I raise my goblet. It is a gift from my supplier, Hiram king of Tyre, and unlike the other goblets I have in my possession, this one is made of fine glass, with minute air bubbles floating in it. With a big splash I fill it up to the rim with red, aromatic wine. In it I dip a glistening, ruddy cherry, and offer it to her, with a flowery toast.

"For you," I say. "With my everlasting love!"

Bathsheba takes the goblet from my hand, and raises it to her lips. "Love, everlasting?" she says, raising an eyebrow. "What does that mean, in this place?"

I hesitate to ask, "What place is that?"

"This court," she says, with a slight curtsy, "where the signature feature is a harem, which is as big as the king is endowed with glory."

"Glory is a good thing," say I, lowering my voice. "But sometimes it is better to meet in the shadows."

"Especially," she says, matching her voice to mine, "when there are so many others."

"Here we are," say I. "It's just us."

"Really," says Bathsheba, sipping her wine and ever so delightfully, licking her lips. "It must be a special night, then! Just you and me, and no one else, no one else at all."

Yet I cannot avoid feeling the presence of someone other than me in her thoughts, perhaps her husband, Uriah, who is one of my mighty soldiers and the most trusty of them. Earlier today he must have received his transfer orders to join the cavalry in the eastern hills, where he would be stationed outside the city of Rabbah.

I have a catch in my throat as I tell her, "I'm so glad you came."

Bathsheba lifts her eyes and looks straight at me.

"Really," she says, in her most velvety tone. "You mean, I had a choice in this matter?"

Her question stumps me at first, because how can I admit that she is right, so right in asking it? Instead I just shrug.

"You do have a choice," I say at last. "And I hope you'll make it."

"I'm so glad to hear that," says Bathsheba. "With that ape, I mean, that bodyguard of yours knocking so loudly, so rudely, and for such a long time at my door, I had my doubts about it."

"You can go, if you wish," I stress, with a reluctant tone. "But I wish you wouldn't. Stay with me, tonight."

Bathsheba picks the stem of the red cherry, and takes little bites out of it. In her pleasure she hums, and smacks her lips. Then she raises the goblet to my lips, letting me take in the aroma. I do, and then I take a long gulp.

With a slight sway of her hips Bathsheba walks past me, knowing I cannot take my eyes off of her. She wanders about my chamber as if she were the one owning it.

"You've been brought here by my order," I whisper to her, across the space. "But I am the one held captive."

Excerpt: The Edge of Revolt

A t last, "Decisive action may be easy for a king," I tell her. "But as a father I must weigh every word I speak, because in the future it may leave a scar upon the hearts of my children."

Somewhat reluctantly she says, "I understand."

"I hope you do," say I. "They are, all of them, my flesh and blood."

"Then, act as a king," she says. "Not as a father. Name the one who will succeed you, the one who—in your judgement—may become a better ruler than the others."

I have to admit, "I have yet to make up my mind," which fills her eyes with worry. She knows all too well that Solomon, being the younger son, has less of a change to win my favor.

"Decide," she says. "And make your wishes known. That in itself may bring about a change, a peaceful transition of power. Otherwise, I'm afraid there will be mayhem. It will start at sunrise."

I let go of her hand, because to say my next sentence I must not lean on anyone.

But before I can muster my pride, and take air in my lungs, and clear my throat to state, in my most regal tones, "I am still the king, am I not," I find myself staggering. In the next instant, there I am, a heap of arms and legs spilled on the floor, twisting in agony from the sudden chill overtaking me.

I reach up, trying to breathe her name. And I wonder what this suffering may look like, to her and to a heavenly city watching over me, floating silent and forlorn on the hill.

Overhead, a cloud breaks off from the others and moves in a new direction. Its wooly, dim grays are drifting across. I squint, rub my eyes. Now, in a separate layer, another image starts floating past: the way she looked, right here on this roof, when we came out of these doors the very first time.

I remember: scattered petals flew off, swirling in the glow around her long, silky hair that started cascading under her, onto the tile floor. In the background, a vine of roses twisted over the wooden lattice and into it. Between its diagonal slats I saw a diamond here, a diamond there of the heavens. I wondered then about the black void that was gaping upon us, dotted by a magical glint of starlight.

Separated from her by the thought of a kiss I sensed her heat, and the gust of air, which was sweetly scented by roses and by her flesh—but I could not tell if the breath between us was hers or mine. Which is when I knew, for the first time in my life, that she would always be part of my essence. I would be part of hers.

Accidentally the goblet, which she had set down next to her, tipped over and some of the wine spilled over her hip. The crisp sound of breaking glass rang in my ear. It marked the moment, from which I could not turn back. Never would I be able to put it out of my mind.

Yes, this was my fault: taking a woman that belonged to another. Soon after came the blunder: bringing her husband,

Uriah, back from the front, that he may sleep with her, which would have explained her pregnancy ever so conveniently.

And when that did not go as planned, then came another mistake, the worst of all: sending him back to the battlefield, with my sealed letter in hand, arranging for his death.

All the while, my boys were learning their own lessons—not from my psalms but from my deeds. One error begets another, each one bringing a new calamity over me, over my family, and over this entire land. Sin followed by execution, followed by revolt, escape, execution, revolt...

Had I known back then the results of the results of my mistake, the curse looming over my life ever since that time, would I still choose to do it?

Bathsheba tries to raise me to my feet. Her fragrance brings back to me the sunny, warm hues of spring. The fears, the doubts flee away when we are that close. I adore the way she calls my name, the way she sighs. With every sweet word I fall deeper into her eyes.

How can love be a mistake? In my passion for her—then as now—what choice do I have?

I want to tell her, "Let me close my eyes. Let me remember."

Excerpt: Overkill

E d lies still on the sidewalk, his eyelids open but unflinching. The only thing about him that moves are the lapels of his corduroy coat, flapping slightly this way and that across his neck as the wind floats chilly feelers over his body.

Timmy gasps—but his eyes are not tearful, not yet. In that second, when time slows, the driver side door is swaying with an annoying noise. With each squeak, the child takes a gulp of air as if about to ask, "Dad, will you get up? Will you grab the door handle?"

No blood is visible, at first. So, I too allow myself to wonder: Will Ed climb back into his seat, dust off his shoulders, and wave goodbye to his son, before driving away?

I expect him to do so. Almost.

Until another round of gunshots blasts the air.

Without even thinking, I push Timmy down to the asphalt, which is quite easy because he's such a skinny child and utterly in shock. Then I land hard on my elbows beside him and push a hand against his chest until he crawls backwards, until he butts against his father's car. It casts a shadow over him. At the moment, there is no better place to hide.

Up on the pavement, a short distance from us, blood starts puddling around Ed's shoulder. I try to block Timmy from seeing it.

He shakes his head, still in disbelief.

Please, God, no. This can't be true.

Everything around us is in a state of utter confusion. The sidewalk is strewn with abandoned backpacks, as some pupils are running for their lives. Others cower behind a bush or a car. One uses his flimsy umbrella as a shield.

A teacher cries out to him, "Duck!"

And another teacher, by the gate of the school, yells, "Run! Get inside! Get down, crawl under your desks! And for Heaven's sake, stay away from the windows!"

A couple of parents attempt getting out of their cars to pull their children to safety, but at the sound of shooting they drop to their knees with empty arms.

Next to me, Timmy turns onto his stomach, mashes his nose against the tire, and wedges himself, somehow, between the curb and the Ford. Then he crawls under it toward the rear bumper, making room for me, too.

I try to cock my head up from the damp surface. Looking at the scene from under the belly of a car is a whole different experience. Someone stands at the other side of the car, and all I can see is his sneakers, socks, and the hem of his coat, flaring at its bottom. Also, the muzzle of his gun. For a heartbeat, before dark clouds close in, it glints in the sunlight.

I reach over and clamp a hand over Timmy's mouth to prevent him from screaming, from drawing the killer's attention. A hail of bullets rains down, sparking off the front bumper.

Timmy tenses up. His breath trembles as it escapes my touch. I must protect him. I must bring him back safely to his mother.

The edge of the curb gouges into my back. I adjust, I turn over. Now it presses against my belly.

I must not lose this child, either.

Now, the killer kicks the grill of the car, then jams his weapon, hard, into the front window. I know it by seeing only one of his feet on the ground and by the sound of cracking. It reverberates all over as the car shakes. Shards of glass come pinging against the asphalt and stab at my fingers.

Why is he wasting his time—at the risk of being identified, or even caught—on an empty car, when all around us, juicier targets come into his view?

Excerpt: Virtually Lace

E ven before Michael spotted the body, the idea of creating a simulation of the scene occurred to him. At sunset, the panoramic view of Laguna Beach was awe-inspiring. He wondered if he could render it convincingly in his model, the virtual reality model which he had been developing in the back of his garage for months, until the recent acquisition of his software by a military ops company.

Could beauty be taken apart without loss of emotional impact? Could its data be synthesized, somehow, into a lifelike experience? In short, could he apply his analytical skills to fool his own senses?

For now, these were purely academic questions. They occupied his mind, which helped him forget his loneliness. Michael brought his car to a stop at the corner of Cliff Drive and let it maneuver by itself into a tight parking spot. In all probability, this evening would be uneventful, or so he thought. It was the end of April. He had nothing to do and no one to do it with.

Sitting there awhile, lost in his thoughts, how was he to know that in the coming days he was going to revisit this place, starting at this particular intersection, to examine every possible angle, every conceivable point of view?

The shadow of the lamppost grew longer. It prowled over to the pavement on the other side, where it lost its sharpness. The evening breeze turned overhead with a shriek, only to fall into a whoosh. Michael imagined it whispering, of all things, of murder at dusk. What a crazy idea! Where did that come from?

At 8:03pm came the sound of footfalls. A teenage girl was walking down the street so fast that the uneven click of her heels was already passing him by, leaving a faint whiff of perfume. No, that must have been some other fragrance, perhaps the saltiness of the sea, drifting over the sweetness of creek milkweeds and Belladonna lilies.

Where had he seen her before?

By the time he got out of the car, the girl had already crossed to the other side. With each step, the white dress whipped across her legs and fluttered, fold upon fold, in the cold wind.

His soles beat an echo in the empty street. He didn't mind the occasional squeak, because he had just bought them.

Electric lights buzzed in the buildings behind him, and foxtail ferns hissed, swaying along the trail. Her shadow flitted over the shrubs, falling farther and farther out of reach.

Before reaching the bend, she glanced over her shoulder and for a heartbeat, met his eyes. In some ways she reminded him of his ex-girlfriend, Ash, whom he hadn't seen since the *incident*. What was it that drew him to this girl? Why was he looking, time and again, to save a damsel in distress?

There was a certain quality about that look, which he couldn't put into words. Anguish? No, it was more acute than that. The closest he could name it was fear.

Excerpt: The Music of Us

My son, Ben, has been gone for a month now, staying in some youth hostel in Rome. If I call him, if I stumble into revealing how scared I am that his mother is losing her mind, he may listen. He may heed my fears, grudgingly, and come back here, not even knowing how to offer his support to me. Should I ask for it?

The last thing I wish to do is lean on him for help. He is not strong enough, and whatever the problem may be with her, I can grit my teeth and handle it, somehow, all by myself. Besides, I pray for a spontaneous change in her. I mean, her memory may take a turn for the better just as quickly as it has deteriorated.

Given this hope I decide that for now I will not schedule the head X-Ray that her doctor recommended for her. I figure she has been through so many checkups, so many exams to rule out depression, vitamin B deficiency, and a long list of other possible ailments, all of which has been in vain.

So far, the results have failed to produce a conclusive diagnosis, and this new X-Ray will be no different, because from what I have read, Alzheimer's disease can be determined only through autopsy, by linking clinical measures with an examination of brain tissue. So this new medical hypothesis is just that: a hypothesis. One that cannot be proven; one that cannot go away. An ever-present threat.

Perhaps all she needs is rest. Time, I tell myself. I must give her time. Meanwhile I resolve to keep her condition secret from everyone, especially from my son. Let him enjoy his time away from home, his independence.

Since his departure I called him only once, three weeks ago, and said little, except for blurting out the mundane, "How's Rome?"

"Great," he said vaguely, adding no particulars.

I could not help myself from asking. "So, what about your plans?"

"What about them?"

"D'you have any?"

"For now I have none," he admitted, and immediately changed the subject. "How's mom?"

"Fine."

"Is she?"

"She is," I lied, hoping that the sound of my voice would not betray the tensing of my muscles, the tightening of my jaws.

"Oh good," he said. "Really, really good."

There is only one thing more difficult than talking to Ben, and that is writing to him. Amazingly, having to conceal what his mother is going through makes every word—even on subjects unrelated to her—that much harder. I find myself oppressed by my own self-imposed discipline, the discipline of silence.

And what can I tell him, really? That I keep digging into the past, mining its moments, trying to piece them together this way and that, dusting off each memory of Natasha, of how we were, the highs and lows of the music of us, to find out where the problem may have started?

To him, that may seem like an exercise in futility. For me, it is a necessary process of discovery, one that is as tormenting as it is delightful. If the dissonance in our life would fade away, so will the harmony.

Sometimes I go as far back as the moment we first met, when I was a soldier and she—a star, brilliant yet illusive. Natasha was a riddle to me then, and to this day, with all the changes she has gone through, she still is.

I often wonder: can we ever understand, truly understand each other—soldier and musician, man and woman, one heart and another? Will we ever again dance together to the same beat? Is there a point where we may still touch?

Uvi Poznansky

Excerpt: Dancing with Air

Overcome, suddenly, by exhaustion, Natasha stepped out of my embrace and plopped onto her suitcase. "Ma came to say goodbye, " she said. "I saw her across from me, as we left the shore. She was offering a prayer, tears running down her cheeks. Then, once out to sea, the Germans fired at us."

"Really? What happened?"

"The ships, they took up their positions in the convoy and plodded ahead. Straightaway, two of them were lost. One ran aground. The other, suffering from engine trouble, turned back to the harbor. And as for us I thought that was the end."

I shuddered at the thought.

"This journey," said Natasha, "it was more challenging than anything I've gone through in the past. Even watching Papa during his last months was easier, in a way, because back then I was on the outside, observing his pain."

I waited for her to continue.

After a slight reflection, she added, "I could only guess what was happening to him, I mean, the ways his illness drained his mind, the ways he suffered. But now, I wasn't an observer. I lived it, Lenny! Everyone on board—including me—was going through the same fear, the same hardship."

I could not help but ask her, "What were you thinking, putting yourself at risk?"

In reply, she rose to her feet. "For this very moment," she said, clinging to me, "I would go through it all over again."

I took a step back, to stress, "Your Mama, she's beside herself with worry, and as for me—"

"You talked to her?" asked Natasha, her eyes twinkling. "Of course you did, how else would you know to wait here for me? She doesn't get it—"

"And neither do I!"

"But Lenny, it's so simple! I missed you—"

"That's no reason, Natasha, for what you've done. Why leave home, especially now, when we're at war? If you love me, keep yourself safe, if only for my sake! Why, why put your life at risk —"

"Perhaps," she said, "I'm not looking for safety! Have you ever thought of that? Perhaps something else is more important to me."

"Like what?"

"I can't continue to depend on others, Lenny, the way I've done all my life. This is my time to change, to demand new things of myself, even if they happen to frighten me, even if I'm scared out of my mind."

"Not sure I understand—"

"Please try, Lenny."

"What is it you want?"

"Just this: to stop leaning on those closest to me."

"You could've done that back home, couldn't you?"

"That's the place where I'm being taken care of, to the point of feeling stuck. Worse than that: suffocated. Someone, usually Mama, drives me to where I need to be. Someone points me to the dressing room, calls me to the stage. I'm nothing more than a mechanical doll. All I do is respond."

"You do much more than that! You excite audiences, Natasha! And to me, you're an inspiration—"

"Yes, you admire the way I play, but in truth music is the only thing for which Papa trained me."

"You're too critical of yourself," I said.

To which she said, "No, Lenny. I've seen him decline, seen him lose his mind, and if—if, like him, I'll ever lose mine—how in the world will I recover? How will I find my way, when I've never developed the skill to do so?"

I lowered my head before her.

"Never," I said, "until now."

"Exactly," said Natasha. "Until now."

And a moment later, blotting the corner of her eye, where a tear was forming, she whispered to me, "Come closer, Lenny, snuggle up, but never, ever let me lean on you."

Excerpt: Twisted

He turns to me with a sly look. To my surprise, his smile—even with those sharp fangs—is quite endearing.

"Job's wife, I presume? Hallelujah! I have been expecting you for quite a long while," says Satan. His voice is sweet. He must have sung in a choir in his youth, because in some ways he sounds as pious as my husband. "Shame, shame, shame on you," he wags his finger. "You sure made me wait, didn't you..."

And without allowing time for an answer, he brings a magnifying glass to his bloodshot eye. Enlarged, his pupil is clearly horizontal and slit-shaped.

Which makes me feel quite at home with him, because so are the pupils of the goats in the herds we used to own.

Meanwhile, Satan unfolds a piece of paper and runs his finger through some names listed there. Then, with a gleam of satisfaction he marks a checkbox there, right in the middle of the crinkled page. At once, a whiff of smoke whirls in the air.

Satan blows off a few specks of charred paper, folds the thing and tucks it into his breast pocket, somewhere in his wool. Cashmere, I ask myself? Really? In this heat?

Back home, when I would count my gold coins, this was something I craved with a passion... It would keep me warm during the long winter nights...

Then, without even bothering to look at me, Satan says, "I swear, madam, you look lovely tonight."

For a moment I am grateful that my husband is among the living. Or so I think. Nowadays, influenced by the elders, he regards swearing as a mortal sin, as bad as cursing. He even plugs his ears, for no better reason than to avoid hearing it. But if you ask me, I swear: without a bit of blasphemy, language would utterly dull, and fit for nothing but endless prayer. Sigh.

Strangely, Satan does not frighten me that much anymore. And so, swaying on my hip bones, I strut out of the cave in his direction. I feel an odd urge to fondle his horns. Along the path toward him I make sure to suck in my belly, because in the company of a gentleman, even a corpse is entitled to look her best.

Books by Uviart

Coma Confidential

(Volume I of *Ash Suspense Thrillers with a Dash of Romance*)
Kindle: B07L92YHST Paperback: 978-1791691592

Overkill

(Volume II of *Ash Suspense Thrillers with a Dash of Romance*)
Kindle: B084GDK156 Paperback: 979-8644328192

Overdose

(Volume III of *Ash Suspense Thrillers with a Dash of Romance*)
Kindle: B07VP4S6PK Paperback: 978-1086703665

Overdue

(Volume IV of *Ash Suspense Thrillers with a Dash of Romance*)
Kindle: B08S724T4G Paperback: 979-8599499671

Uvi Poznansky

Ash Suspense Thrillers: Trilogy

(Volume I-III of *Ash Suspense Thrillers with a Dash of Romance*)

Kindle: B0893MJNSY Paperback: 979-8648269644

Virtually Lace

(Volume I of *High-Tech Crime Solvers*)

Kindle: B07L968RXD Paperback: 978-1790407187

My Own Voice

(Volume I of *Still Life with Memories*)

Kindle: B013TA3FBS Paperback: 978-0984993215

The White Piano

(Volume II of *Still Life with Memories*)

Kindle: B013TAU7L4 Paperback: 978-1517049447

The Music of Us

(Volume III of *Still Life with Memories*)

Kindle: B013TCYWHC Paperback: 978-0-9849932-9-1

Dancing with Air

(Volume IV of *Still Life with Memories*)

Kindle: B01I4ENROY Paperback: 978-1536896534

Marriage before Death

(Volume V of *Still Life with Memories*)

Kindle: B0746NW5CD Paperback: 978-1974001736

Apart from Love

(*Still Life with Memories Bundle I*)

Kindle: B006WPITP0 Paperback: 978-0-9849932-0-8

Apart from War

(*Still Life with Memories Bundle II*)

Kindle: B07MMZLD7Z Paperback: 978-1792131592

Uvi Poznansky

Rise to Power

(Volume I of *The David Chronicles*)

Kindle: B00H6PMZ0U Paperback: 978-0-9849932-4-6

A Peek at Bathsheba

(Volume II of *The David Chronicles*)

Kindle: B00LEPPDV6 Paperback: 978-0-9849932-7-7

The Edge of Revolt

(Volume III of *The David Chronicles*)

Kindle: B00Q5WVKA6 Paperback: 978-0984993284

The David Chronicles: Trilogy

(Volume I-III of *The David Chronicles*)

Kindle: B00QYGF6WG Paperback: 978-1797440699

The David Chronicles: Art

(Volume IV-XI of *The David Chronicles*)

Kindle: B08YWSH7HC Paperback: 979-8721612886

Inspired by Art: Fighting Goliath

(Art book. Volume IV of *The David Chronicles*)

Kindle: B01MSBNSE4   Paperback 978-1797726212

Inspired by Art: Fall of a Giant

(Art book. Volume V of *The David Chronicles*)

Kindle: B01MSBS82Q   Paperback: 978-1092307765

Inspired by Art: Rise to Power

(Art book. Volume VI of *The David Chronicles*)

Kindle: B01N2786VX   Paperback: 978-1092263207

Inspired by Art: A Peek at Bathsheba

(Art book. Volume VII of *The David Chronicles*)

Kindle: B01MUFS9OA   Paperback: 978-1092306225

Inspired by Art: The Edge of Revolt

(Art book. Volume VIII of *The David Chronicles*)

Kindle: B01N6ZG0W8   Paperback: 978-1091306158

Inspired by Art: The Last Concubine

(Art book. Volume IX of *The David Chronicles*)

Kindle: B01N2AXQP2   Paperback: 978-1092302715

A Favorite Son

Kindle: B00AUZ3LGU Paperback: 978-0-9849932-5-3

Twisted

Kindle: B00D7Q3IY4

Paperback: 978-0984993260 Nook: 2940151689588

Home

(Poetry)

Kindle: B00960TE3Y

Paperback: 978-09849932-3-9 Nook: 2940151729468

Can We Still Love

(Poetry)

Kindle: B0GV3G23V4 Paperback: B0GY8Q1Y9Z

Virtually Yummy: Recipes that Inspire

(Cookbook)

Kindle: B085BDNDM5 Nook: 2940163988655

Apple: id1501182051 Kobo: 9781393589853

בית

(Poetry in Hebrew)
Paperback: 978-1494920968

Apple: id1302908918 Kobo: 9781540199966

Jess and Wiggle

Kindle: B013D1W0SM Paperback: 978-1494920968

Now I Am Paper

Kindle: B00YQS4O72 Paperback: 978-1494919429

www.ingramcontent.com/pod-product-compliance
Lightning Source LLC
Chambersburg PA
CBHW022047170626
46808CB00003B/1385